# ANIMAL
## CRACKERS

## HOT DOG HARRIS

# ROSE IMPEY ★ SHOO RAYNER

ORCHARD BOOKS

ORCHARD BOOKS
338 Euston Road, London NW1 3BH
*Orchard Books Australia*
Hachette Children's Books
Level 17/207 Kent Street, Sydney NSW 2000

First published by Orchard Books in 1993
This edition published in 2008

Text © Rose Impey 1993
Illustrations © Shoo Rayner 2002

The rights of Rose Impey to be identified as the author and
Shoo Rayner to be identified as the illustrator of this Work
have been asserted by them in accordance with the
Copyright, Designs and Patents Act, 1988.

A CIP catalogue record for this book is available from the British Library.

ISBN 978 1 40830 295 8

1 3 5 7 9 10 8 6 4 2
Printed in China

Orchard Books is a division of Hachette Children's Books,
an Hachette Livre UK company.
www.hachettelivre.co.uk

# Hot Dog Harris

It's easy to lose things
down the back of a sofa:
odd socks,
half-eaten jelly babies,
the remote control
for the television.
Even a set of teeth –
if they were loose.

But a dog would be
difficult to lose.
*Unless* it was Hot Dog Harris,
"the smallest dog in the world".
Then it would be easy.

Hot Dog was a Yorkshire Terrier.
He lived in Barnsley
with Mr and Mrs Harris
and their son Harold
and their daughter Hattie
and their grandad, old Mr Harris.

Old Mr Harris didn't think much
of Hot Dog.
"You call that a dog!" he said.
"It looks like a wig on legs."

Oh, Grandad!

But the rest of the family
liked Hot Dog.
They liked small dogs.
The smaller the better.
And Hot Dog was
a "Tom Thumb" of a dog.

Hot Dog was small
enough to sit on
Mr Harris's hand,

to sleep in Mrs Harris's hat,

to fit in Hattie's
pencil case,

to have a bath
in Harold's
football cup.

Hot Dog was no bigger
than a bar of soap

or a bag of chips

or a...hot dog!

He would hardly have filled one.

Hot Dog was *so* small
everyone had to be
very careful around him.

Old Mr Harris had to be careful
where he sat down.

Mrs Harris had to be careful
when she hoovered the carpet.

Mr Harris had to be careful
every time he blew his nose.

Harold had to be careful
whenever he put on
his football boots.

Hattie had to be careful to look *before* she jumped into bed.

They all had to be careful
not to let Hot Dog
out of the house.
He was so small
anything might happen!

But Hot Dog wasn't afraid.
There was nothing
he would have liked better
than to explore the world.
Hot Dog was always looking
for a way to get out.

Sometimes he found it.

"Eee, that dog will be
the death of me," said Mr Harris.
"He'll be the death of himself,"
said Mrs Harris.

And one time he nearly was.

It was the day the plumber came
to mend the washing machine.
Behind it was a hole.
Not a big hole –
but big enough.
Hot Dog set out
to explore the world.

The first place he explored
was next door's garden.
Next door there was a patio
and a pond
and children with lots of toys.

Hot Dog went for a ride
on a roller-skate.
He didn't know
he could roller-skate.
He roller-skated right into the pond.

Hot Dog didn't know
he could swim either.
But he soon found out.
He swam round and round in circles.

Four fat goldfish swam
round and round too.

They looked hungry.
Hot Dog tried to bark
but he swallowed water.
He nearly drowned.
Getting out wasn't easy either,
but he did it.

Hot Dog had explored water
and he *didn't* like it.

Hot Dog shook himself
and walked down the road.
The next place he explored
was the park.
It was a big, wide open space.
There were dogs everywhere.
Some of them were big enough
to eat Hot Dog for breakfast
and still feel hungry.

Town Park
Dogs must
be kept on
a lead

But Hot Dog was brave.
*And* he was fast
on his feet.
*And* he had sharp teeth.
Some of those dogs
didn't know what had bitten them.

But Hot Dog had explored
the wide open spaces
and he didn't like those *either*.

Hot Dog walked on until he came
to the canal bank.
It was a long way
for a dog with very short legs.

Hot Dog was looking for
somewhere to rest.
He found a hole.

Hot Dog explored the hole.
It went deep underground.
There was a strong smell
and it wasn't a dog smell.

Hot Dog came out backwards –
very fast.

After him came a water rat.
It was the same size as him –
but its teeth were bigger.
Hot Dog ran off.

Hot Dog had explored underground
and he didn't like that *either.*

By now Hot Dog was worn out.
He wished he was at home
in Mrs Harris's hat.

Just then a bird flew
out of a tree.
A big black and white bird.
It was a magpie.

It spotted Hot Dog's collar.
Magpies like bright things.
The magpie carried Hot Dog
up in the air.

**33**

It carried Hot Dog
over the canal
and the park.
Over streets
and houses
and gardens.

Hot Dog had never been
flying before.
He didn't think he liked it.

Hot Dog began to feel sick.
He wriggled and jiggled.
He snapped his jaws
and barked at the magpie.

The magpie opened its beak
and Hot Dog fell
down

and down

and down.

Luckily Hot Dog landed in a tree.
Unluckily it was a tall tree.

Hot Dog had explored the sky
and he liked it least of all.
He sat on a branch and *howled!*

The children in the next garden
heard him howling.
They told their mum.
Their mum told the lady next door.
The lady next door was...
Mrs Harris.

Mrs Harris was in a state.
All the family was in a state.
They couldn't find Hot Dog.
They had looked in all the
usual places.
Even down the back of the sofa.

When they saw Hot Dog up the tree
they phoned the fire brigade.

The firemen came with their
fire engine.

The firemen often rescued
*cats* from trees.
They had never rescued
a *dog* before.
No one could work out
*how* he had got there
in the first place.

"That dog!" said Mr Harris.
"He gets everywhere.
You mark my words:
he won't be happy climbing trees,
he'll be climbing mountains next."

"At least he'd keep
someone's head warm,"
said old Mr Harris.
"The first wig up Everest."
"Oh, Grandad!" said Hattie.

But the tiny explorer
was already asleep
and dreaming.

# Crack-A-Joke

What do you get
if you cross a dog
with a jeep?
**A Land Rover!**

What kind of dogs
sit by the fire?
**Hot dogs!**

How do you stop your dog barking
in the back seat of the car?
**Put him in the
front seat!**

# You'll be howling with laughter!

What do you get if you cross a dog with a telephone?
**A golden receiver!**

What did the lazy flea say?
**Shall we walk, or catch a dog?**

Doctor, Doctor, I feel like a dog!

How long has this been going on?

Since I was a puppy!

# ANIMAL
## CRACKERS

## COLLECT ALL THE
## ANIMAL CRACKERS BOOKS!

| | | |
|---|---|---|
| A Birthday for Bluebell | 978 1 40830 293 4 | £4.99 |
| Too Many Babies | 978 1 40830 294 1 | £4.99 |
| Hot Dog Harris | 978 1 40830 295 8 | £4.99 |
| Sleepy Sammy | 978 1 40830 296 5 | £4.99 |
| Precious Potter | 978 1 40830 297 2 | £4.99 |
| Phew Sidney | 978 1 40830 298 9 | £4.99 |
| Open Wide Wilbur | 978 1 40830 299 6 | £4.99 |
| We Want William | 978 1 40830 300 9 | £4.99 |

All priced at £4.99

Orchard Colour Crunchies are available from all good bookshops, or can be
ordered direct from the publisher:
Orchard Books, PO BOX 29, Douglas IM99 1BQ
Credit card orders please telephone 01624 836000
or fax 01624 837033 or visit our internet site: www.orchardbooks.co.uk
or e-mail: bookshop@enterprise.net for details.
To order please quote title, author and ISBN
and your full name and address.
Cheques and postal orders should be made payable to 'Bookpost plc.'
Postage and packing is FREE within the UK
(overseas customers should add £2.00 per book).
Prices and availability are subject to change.